HELLO! WELCOME TO THE FABUMOUSE WORLD OF THE THEA SISTERS!

Hi, I'm Thea Stilton, Geronimo Stilton's sister! I am a special reporter for The Rodent's Gazette, the most famouse newspaper on Mouse Island. I love traveling and meeting new mice all over the world, like the Thea Sisters. These five friends have helped me out with my adventures. Let me introduce you to these fabumouse young mice!

Colette has a real passion for fashion. She loves to design her own clothes in her favorite color, pink.

Violet loves studying and learning new things. She is a fan of classical music and dreams of becoming a famouse violinist someday.

Pamela loves pizza so much she eats it for breakfast. She is a skilled mechanic who can fix just about any motor she gets her paws on.

PAULINA is shy and loves to read about faraway places. But she loves traveling to those places even more.

Nicky is from the Australian Outback, where she developed a love of nature and the environment. This outdoors-loving mouse is always on the move.

Scholastic Inc.

ISBN 978-0-545-78905-9

Based on an original idea by Elisabetta Dami.

www.geronimostilton.com

Published by Scholastic Inc., 557 Broadway, New York, NY 10012.

Text by Thea Stilton
Original title *Cinque amiche per un musical*
Cover by Giuseppe Facciotto
Illustrations by Chiara Balleello and Francesco Castelli
Graphics by Yuko Egusa

Special thanks to Tracey West
Translated by Anna Pizzelli
Interior design by Becky James

12 11 10 9 8 7 6 18 19 20/0

Printed in the U.S.A. 40
First printing, January 2015

WHAT WILL IT BE?

It was a sunny morning, and the students at Mouseford Academy were busier than ever. School would be ending soon, and everyone was talking about the same thing: what would the end-of-the-year show be?

This year was especially exciting, because it was the first year of the DEPARTMENT OF ARTS, MUSIC, and **DRAMA**. Headed by Professor Camille Ratyshnikov, the department was popular with many of the students — including the five THEA SISTERS.

"The show is only a month away!" said Paulina excitedly.

Paulina and the other Thea Sisters were

headed across campus to clean up the old greenhouse.

"Well, I heard that the professors are being very secretive about what show we're doing," said blond-haired Colette, who carried a box of small rosebushes.

"But we do know that it will be a MUSICAL," said Violet, who played the violin. "Won't that be amazing? There will be singing, dancing, DRAMA . . ."

"Tryouts will be INTENSE!" said Pam.

"Definitely," agreed Nicky. "I need to practice my dance moves. But first, we need to clean up this greenhouse for Professor Rattcliff."

"It will look so fabumouse when we're done," said Colette. "I can't wait to plant these roses."

"These LIGHTS will look beautiful," said Violet.

"And so will these Flags, if I can get them apart," added Pam, looking at the tangled decorations she was carrying.

"The decorations are a great idea,"

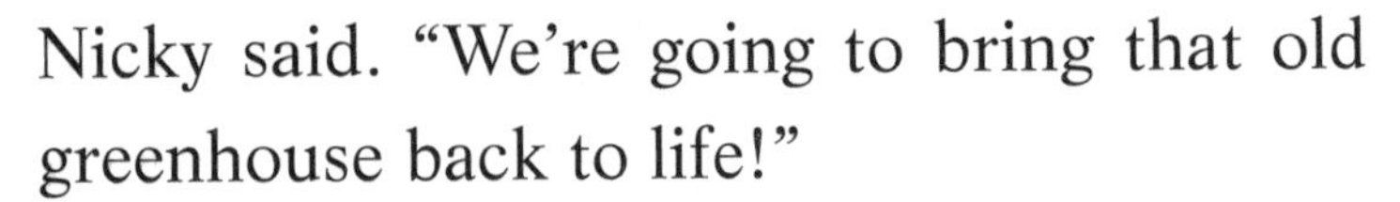

Nicky said. "We're going to bring that old greenhouse back to life!"

Just then, Professor Rosalyn Plié came walking down the path toward them. The professor of DANCE at the academy, she was part of the team involved in planning the musical. She had a worried look on her snout and did not seem to notice the Thea Sisters.

"Good morning, Professor!" Nicky said.

"Oh, good morning!" replied Professor Plié, stopping in front of them. "I didn't mean to ignore you. I'm on my way to a meeting for the big year-end show, and I have a lot on my mind."

"Is it true that it will be a MUSICAL?" asked Violet.

"And if it is, can you give us a hint what it is?" Pam asked. "*The Sound of Cheddar*? *Phantom of the Cheese Factory*?"

"Yes, please tell us the title!" Colette joined in.

Professor Plié sighed. How could she confess to these excited students that she did not have the faintest idea?

AN INSPIRING MESS

"I'm sorry, but I can't tell you," Professor Plié replied. "You see, the meeting is about to start and we —"

"Sensational news!" a voice interrupted.

It was Tanja, the president of the Lizard Club, coming out of nowhere like a bolt of LIGHTNING.

"The professors are about to decide — WHOOPS!" She tripped over Pam's tangled flags. Then she knocked into Nicky and Violet.

Whoops!

Embarrassed, Tanja immediately got back on her paws. "Sorry! I just came to tell you that they're about to choose —"

"THE MUSICAL!" the Thea Sisters finished, grinning. They may have collided with Tanja, but that didn't dampen their excitement about the show!

"That's what I was trying to tell you," said Professor Plié. "We're supposed to choose the musical today, but to be honest, we don't have any great ideas yet. It needs to be a fun show, with colorful sets and UPBEAT MUSIC. I just haven't found any inspiration yet!"

As she spoke, Professor Plié noticed the scene in front of her. Holey cheese — Tanja had caused quite a MESS! None of the Thea Sisters were hurt, but they looked awfully funny.

The tangled flags were wrapped around Pam's hair. It reminded the professor of a **LION'S** ruffled-up mane.

Nicky was covered in **STRAW** that had fallen out of her broom, and she looked like a **SCARECROW**!

Violet sat unhappily with an empty bucket on her head, like a sulking **TIN MAN**.

"I've got it — we can perform **The Wonderful Wizard of Oz**!" Professor Plié cried.

She hugged Tanja **warmly**. "Thank you! That was just the inspiration I needed!" Then she ***RAN*** down the path, leaving the students speechless behind her.

The Wonderful Wizard of Oz

Published in 1910, this famouse book was written by American author L. Frank Baum. The book tells the story of Dorothy, who is carried to the amazing Land of Oz by a tornado. While searching for the way home, she meets three special friends: a lion looking for courage, a scarecrow who wants to become smarter, and a tin man who wishes he had a heart.

A STORY OF FRIENDSHIP

The other professors loved Professor Plié's idea to perform *The Wonderful Wizard of Oz*. The next day, they called a meeting in the main hall to share the **news** with the students.

The Thea Sisters sat with Tanja and her best friend, Elly. Colette had brought a **NOTEBOOK** so she could take notes. She **GAZED** around the hall. Ruby Flashyfur and her **friends** Zoe, Connie, and Alicia sat in the front row, as usual.

Ruby's brother, Ryder, and his friends Craig and Shen sat all the way in the back row. They were obviously trying to look **uninterested**,

but Colette knew they were as CURIOUS as everyone else.

The academy's headmaster, Octavius de Mousus, stood up to squeak.

"I have an **ANNOUNCEMENT** to make," he began, and the students quickly quieted down.

Headmaster de Mousus looked around. "Professor Plié has presented us with a MARVEMOUSE idea for our yearly show. We will perform the musical inspired by the book The Wonderful Wizard of Oz!"

The students started squeaking excitedly in hushed whispers. Most of them knew the story well, but several of them looked confused.

The headmaster motioned to Professor Plotfur, who taught drama. He stepped forward. "*The Wonderful Wizard of Oz* is the story of a girl named Dorothy and her fascinating trip to a magic world," he began, waving his paws as he talked. "One day, a tornado sweeps into her small town and whisks her away to a strange land. A good witch tells her that a WONDERFUL WIZARD can help her find her way home."

The students whispered approvingly.

Professor Plotfur went on. "In our version, Dorothy starts walking along a

One day, Dorothy
arrives in a magical world . . .
THE
WONDERFUL
WIZARD
OF OZ

CHEDDAR BRICK ROAD, starting an adventure that will teach her the importance of a COURAGEOUS spirit, a BRILLIANT mind, and a generous heart. But most of all, she learns about the importance of friendship!"

The Thea Sisters smiled at one another. They'd had many adventures together, and their friendship had become **STRONGER** because of those fabumouse experiences.

It seemed like this story had been written just for them!

DOROTHY'S JOURNEY

Professor Plotfur continued the story. "While Dorothy is on the cheddar brick road, she meets three very unique **CHARACTERS**. There is a sweet lion who thought

he was a coward, but finds out that he has **COURAGE** to spare. There is a tin man who would like to have a **heart**, but learns that he is already filled with love and kindness. And finally, there is a scarecrow

who thinks he isn't smart, but ends up using his *intelligence* to solve problems."

Colette took notes on the characters as

Professor Plotfur talked.

"At the end of her journey, Dorothy discovers a great truth before she can go home. The wizard does not have any magic powers. He reminds her that her love for her friends and family is the only magic she needs."

The students were silent as they listened to the story. Only the sound of Colette's pencil filled the hall.

SCRATCH . . . SCRATCH . . .

Professor Plié winked at the Thea Sisters and their friends. Thanks to their FUNNY accident the day before, she had been reminded of the characters of that famouse story!

Professor Camille Ratyshnikov, head of the Department of Arts, Music, and Drama, stepped forward next.

"We only have a month to rehearse, and the auditions will be very **CHALLENGING**," she warned. "Because this show is a musical, our performers will have to excel in Singing and DANCING as well as **ACTING**."

Some of the students groaned. Not everyone was good at all three things!

"This is going to be hard," whispered Nicky.

Professor Plié handed out **FLYERS** with the audition dates and times.

"There will be three stages of auditions," she explained. "The first audition is for

acting and will take place tomorrow with Professor Plotfur."

Professor Plotfur gave a silly bow, and everybody burst out laughing.

"Any student who passes the acting audition will attend my DANCE audition the following day," announced Professor Plié. "And whoever passes those auditions will go to the singing audition with Professor Aria."

Professor Aria waved to the students.

Paulina leaned in to her friends. "Holey cheese!" she whispered. "I'm going to need a lot of CHEESE PIZZA to get through the next three days."

M
MOUSEFORD ACADEMY
AUDITIONS FOR
THE END-OF-THE-YEAR
MUSICAL
THE
WONDERFUL WIZARD
OF OZ
TUESDAY 9:00 a.m., garden:
Acting audition, Professor Robert Plotfur
WEDNESDAY 9:00 a.m., dance hall:
Dance audition, Professor Rosalyn Plié
THURSDAY 9:00 a.m., theater:
Singing audition, Professor Anna Aria

A COLORFUL CAST OF CHARACTERS

The Thea Sisters and Tanja left the room and gathered in the hallway outside. Paulina **SEARCHED** on her tablet for more information about *The Wonderful Wizard of Oz*. She read her findings out loud.

"'Dorothy is the leading character, but she has many friends, as well as some **enemies**,'" she said.

"**THE WICKED WITCH OF THE WEST**!" exclaimed Nicky. "My grandmother* read me a chapter of the book every night before I went to **sleep**. The witch was scary, but those were my favorite parts."

Paulina sighed. "I would read it often to my little sister, Maria. Dorothy reminds

*The Thea Sisters met her in *Thea Stilton and the Mountain of Fire*.

me so much of her! I really miss her."

"**Dorothy** would be a great role to play," said Violet. "But it would be fun if we could each play a role."

Pam had a idea. "I'm not sure if I want

to be onstage. Professor Plotfur was talking to me about doing lighting and SET DESIGN for the play, and I think I'd like to try that."

"You'll be great!" Colette said. "I'm thinking I might stay behind the scenes, too. If I didn't get the role of Dorothy, I wouldn't want to play the wicked WITCH."

Paulina smiled. "Colette, I can't imagine you in that role! The wicked witch is always causing trouble."

"And you have too much fashion sense for that part," added Nicky. "You'd have to wear a long, red wig to cover your blond curls. Plus a black pointy hat, BLACK robes, and GREEN STRIPED socks. That's what the pictures in my book looked like."

Colette nodded. "Definitely not fashion forward!"

Then the friends heard a familiar voice behind them.

"Here you are. I've been looking for you!"

Ruby Flashyfur walked up to them. Her long, red hair hung down her back, and she wore a **BLACK** hat — and **GREEN STRIPED** socks!

"Remind you of anyone?" Nicky whispered to Colette.

A FAIR CHALLENGE?

Ruby smiled and held out her paw.

The Thea Sisters and Tanja were totally squeakless. Why was she being so friendly?

"Last time there was a show, we all wanted to play Juliet in *Mouseo and Juliet*," she reminded them. "And now we all want the role of Dorothy. But I PROMISE, there will be no tricks this time around. May the best mouse win!"

The Thea Sisters looked at one another, SURPRISED. This was not the arrogant Ruby Flashyfur that they all knew. Even Ruby's friends seemed PUZZLED by her friendly behavior.

It will be a fair challenge!

"I'm **happy** to hear that," said Paulina.

"It will be a fair challenge," Ruby continued, "because I am the **best** singer and dancer in the academy. I don't need any **TRICKS** to win the lead this time!"

Then she walked off, **PROUDLY** holding her snout in the air. She had meant what she said. She could feel it in her fur — the role of Dorothy was hers, guaranteed.

Then her **cell phone** rang.

"Hi, Mom," said Ruby.

"I heard about the show," said Ruby's mother, Rebecca Flashyfur. "It's a great opportunity for you to show off your talents. I have already contacted some **FAMOUSE** journalists to interview you on opening night. But you must get that leading role!"

"Don't worry," Ruby promised her. "It's a sure thing this time."

"It had better be," said her mother testily. "I've already told all of my friends that you've got the lead part in the show, and I don't want to look foolish. Take care of your rivals so that nothing can go wrong."

Ruby sighed. She had really wanted to play fair this time. But when her mom put PRESSURE on her, it was hard to say no.

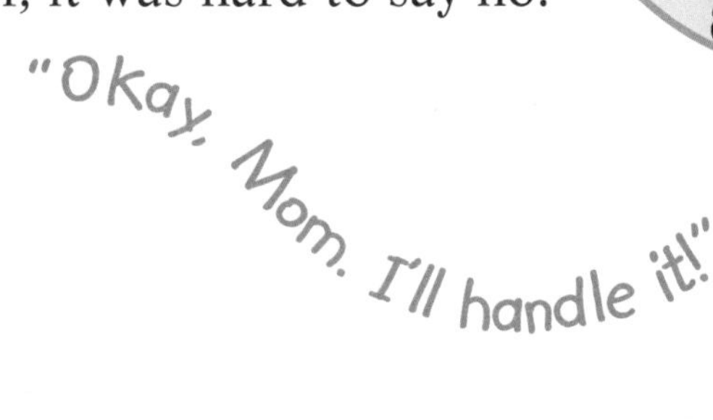

I'M AN ATHLETE, NOT A SINGER!

The boy mice wandered out of the main hall. Shen could not stop talking about the show.

"It's going to be awesome!" he said. "Better than EXTRA-CHEESE PIZZA!"

"Yeah, right," teased Ryder. "You're just excited because you and Pam are going to be working on the lighting and SETS together."

Tall and athletic Craig gave Shen a big pat on the back that almost KNOCKED OVER the smaller mouse. "An entire month working with Pam. That's like your dream come true, right, Shen?"

Shen blushed all the way to the tips of his ears, clearing his throat.

Shen and
Pam!

"What about you, Craig?" Ryder asked. "Are you going to audition?"

This time it was Craig who blushed, and he stuttered. "M-me? No, I'm not into it."

"Come on!" said Shen. "I know you like MUSICALS. You made me watch *Les Mouserables* with you, like, seventeen times."

"It's just . . ." Craig looked uncomfortable. "I can't sing, okay? I get embarrassed and my voice **cracks**."

He started walking BACKWARD, and then . . .

BAM!

He backed up right into Colette! Her notebook **slipped** out of her paws.

"**Oops! Sorry**," Craig mumbled.

Pages of COLORFUL SKETCHES fell out of Colette's notebook. Violet picked them up.

"What are these?" she asked.

Tanja looked at them. "These are amazing DRAWINGS!"

"You were born to be a costume designer, Colette," said Pam as she **EXAMINED** the sketches with a smile on her face.

"That's why your PENCIL kept moving

during the meeting," guessed Violet. Inspired, Colette had been sketching costumes for the show!

Colette shrugged modestly. "They're just sketches, I'm not sure if —"

"Tanja and I took a SEWING class," interrupted Elly, excited. "We can help you make the costumes!"

Tanja nodded. "We should start working on them right away!"

The Thea Sisters and their friends started to walk off, talking about their plans.

"Sorry again, Colette!" Craig called out. He looked

sad and worried.

"So, Craig," Shen resumed. "Are you going to audition or not?"

Craig frowned. "No way! I'm an athlete, not a singer!"

LET'S IMPROVISE!

A large group of students gathered in the campus garden at nine the next morning. It was time for the first audition: acting!

Violet, Nicky, and Paulina were nervous, but their friends encouraged them.

"YOU'LL BE FABUMOUSE!" said Pam, waving as she went off to work on the set design.

"*We'll be thinking of you!*" said Colette, Elly, and Tanja. Then they headed off to the theater to work on the costumes.

Ruby Flashyfur had plans that morning, too: SABOTAGE!

"All right," she said, as the Ruby Crew gathered around her in a circle. "Our goal is to eliminate the Thea Sisters from the audition. Luckily, Pamela and Colette have made it easy for us. I bet they were afraid to audition once they were sure that *I* was trying out."

Purple-haired Zoe grinned. "I knew you weren't SERIOUS about all that 'fair challenge' stuff," she said. "Connie and I have already prepared the PERFECT trick for you."

"It's the best," promised black-haired Connie. She opened her paw to reveal a piece of red candy.

"Ooh, candy!" said blond-haired Alicia. "That looks yummy."

Connie quickly snatched away her paw.

You'll do great!

I wonder what we'll have to do.

"Well, they're not! Their filling is made of SUPER-SPICY pepper cheese!"

Ruby grinned. "Good thinking, Ruby Crew!" she said. "I want to see how the Thea Sisters will be able to talk with FIERY-hot throats!"

Her friends burst out laughing just as Professor Plotfur asked everyone to quiet down.

"One of the most challenging exercises for an actor is improvisation," he began. "That is acting by following what happens in the moment, without a script. And I think a challenge is just what we need today!"

Some of the students GROANED.

"So the theme of our first audition

is **IMPROVISATION**!" Professor Plotfur concluded. "We'll go into the village. Alone, or with a team, you must come up with a sketch. The villagers will be your **AUDIENCE**, and the street will be your **STAGE**. Those of you who manage to get the most **attention** will pass the audition."

Ruby Flashyfur grinned. She had always been the center of attention ever since she was a little mouselet!

This will be easy, she told herself.

Violet, meanwhile, was very **nervous**. It was already difficult for her to get over her shyness onstage. How could she act in front of **strangers** on a street?

"I'll never make it!" she whispered. "I can't act out on the street, in front of everybody. It's too **embarrassing**!"

Paulina hugged her. "You'll make it, Vi. We'll be with you."

Nicky nodded. "You're so **talented**. I know you can do this!"

A LITTLE HELP FROM FRIENDS

Professor Plotfur led the students down the PATH toward the village. Everyone was talking excitedly, trying to think up ideas for sketches. Ryder noticed that one of his friends was lagging behind — CRAIG!

Craig hung back at the campus, sadly staring down at his paws. He wasn't following the crowd.

Ryder tugged on Shen's sleeve. "What's up with Craig?" he asked, pointing. "He's acting really WEIRD."

Shen nodded. "Yeah. He

loves acting, but he seems really afraid of singing."

They heard a voice behind them. "Maybe deep down he wants to try out, but his fear is holding him back."

Shen and Ryder turned around to see Professor Bartholomew Sparkle walking toward them, smiling.

"Do you really think so, Professor Sparkle?" Ryder asked. "Craig has never

been afraid to audition before."

"That's right," Shen confirmed. "He's always so sure of himself. He's the FIRST one to line up for a race, and the FIRST one to step onto the field in a game. He never gets nervous!"

Professor Sparkle nodded. "It's like my grandpaw used to say: 'Even the strongest cheese can MELT when it's hot enough.' Craig just needs to find his CONFIDENCE about singing. Perhaps he needs a little PUSH from his friends."

Then he walked off.

Shen looked at Ryder. "What did he just say? That melted-cheese stuff confused me."

Ryder nodded thoughtfully. "I think I know what to do . . ."

THE SABOTAGE BEGINS!

While Ryder and Shen figured out how to help Craig, Professor Plotfur's group reached the village.

"Come on!" Ruby urged her friends, and she motioned for them to follow her into the town square. "Let's do a DANCE routine. That will get a lot of attention!"

"But we're supposed to be **ACTING**," Zoe reminded her.

"Yeah, well, we can recite lines from the play while we dance," said Ruby. "Just follow my lead."

Every member of the Ruby Crew was a good dancer. And, luckily, they had brought a set of matching outfits with them! A

small crowd of villagers gathered around to WATCH.

"We've got to head down the cheddar brick road," Ruby said.

"Head down the Cheddar Brick Road!" repeated the Ruby Crew.

The crowd clapped their PAWS to the beat. Professor Plotfur approached Ruby and her friends when they had finished.

"That was more dancing than acting, but I give you an A+ for energy," he said. "All four of you **PASS** the audition!"

The Ruby Crew high-pawed one another.

Nicky turned to Violet. "How about a COMEDY routine with me and Paulina?"

Violet shook her head. "I'm still too nervous. You two go. I'll think of something."

Paulina walked toward a store window.

Bravo!

The shopkeeper inside was wiping the glass. Paulina started to copy his movements, as if he were standing in front of a MIRROR.

Then Nicky did the same thing, COPYING the walk of a rodent passing by. Once the villagers caught on, a small crowd gathered around them, laughing.

IT WAS A COMPLETE SUCCESS!

"Nicky and Paulina, you pass!" Professor Plotfur announced.

The Ruby Crew scowled.

"GRR, I AM SO MAD!" Connie growled.

"Don't worry," Ruby told her. "We can still take one of them down."

She walked up to Violet, who was nervously twisting a lock of her long hair.

"You look anxious," Ruby said. "I have just the thing to help you," she said. Then she handed Violet a piece of the RED candy.

"Oh, thank you," Violet said, and popped it in her mouth.

Immediately, her throat began to BURN. It felt like it was on FIRE!

PANICKED, Violet sprinted to the nearest water fountain and GULPED down water.

"Violet, what happened?" Nicky asked.

"Ruby . . . candy . . . hot . . ." Violet gasped.

Professor Plotfur approached. "That was **dramatic**, Violet, but short and, frankly, confusing," he said. "I'm afraid you don't pass the audition."

"But, Professor, she was sabotaged!" Paulina exclaimed.

"Yes, Ruby gave her a **super-spicy** piece of candy!" added Nicky.

Ruby blinked innocently. "Super-spicy? But I just gave her a *throat soother*."

Professor Plotfur frowned. "Violet, would you like to audition again?"

Violet shook her head. "No. I'm not cut out for this kind of audition. I'm just too *shy*!"

A SURPRISE PERFORMANCE

Other students were still auditioning, doing their best to improvise, when a strange group of rodents ran into the village. It was Ryder and Shen, dressed in RUNNING clothes and jogging behind Craig.

"What a great idea, Ryder!" Craig was

saying. "I really needed this mouserific run."

Shen PUFFED and PANTED behind Ryder, but he nodded to his friend. Their plan was working perfectly!

It was Ryder's idea: they could help Craig try out for the audition without him even knowing about it!

The first step of the plan was to get Craig into the village, so Ryder suggested the run. The second step was a little trickier.

As soon as they jogged into the main square, Ryder signaled to Shen as if to say, "Let the show begin!"

Shen spotted two rodents carrying BOXES of fruit and vegetables. They were about to cross Craig's path. So Shen called out to Craig to distract him.

Craig turned his head at the sound of Shen's voice and . . .

BAM!

Craig bumped into the two unlucky rodents, sending apples and lettuce leaves flying everywhere! They showered down on poor Craig.

But that was just the first funny accident that Shen and Ryder set up. They had much more in store for him . . .

HOOOOOONK!
OOOOOOPS!
Splash!

OH-OH!
AAAAARGH!
BRAVO!

"WOO-HOO!"

"BRAVO! ONE MORE TIME!"

"YOU WERE AMAZING!"

After his last fall, Craig landed at the feet of Professor Plotfur. A crowd of loudly clapping rodents had gathered around.

The professor smiled and extended a paw to help him up.

"You and your friends were really very funny," he said. "You played with that classic comic art form, slapstick. Great job. You all pass the acting audition!"

COLETTE'S GOOD NEWS

At the end of the day, Violet, Paulina, and Nicky went to the school stage to check on their friends. They found Pamela happily building SCENERY for the show with Tanja and Elly.

"How did the auditions go?" she asked.

"Good for me and Paulina, but not so good for Violet," Nicky answered. "Ruby played a trick on her and ruined her audition!"

"Typical Ruby!" Pamela exclaimed. "But didn't she promise us a FAIR CHALLENGE this time?"

"So she said," replied Paulina. "But I guess she changed her mind."

"She denied playing the trick, and we

couldn't prove it," Nicky added. "I still say it's not fair!"

"Honestly, it's okay," said Violet. "I enjoyed playing Juliet, but I don't think a MUSICAL is for me. And this way, I can help Colette with the costumes!"

"By the way, where is Colette?" Paulina asked.

Right at that very moment, Colette RUSHED into the auditorium.

"Yes! Yes! Yes!" she exclaimed, twirling around in front of her friends. She held a PINK FOLDER in her hand. "The professors loved our sketches and have decided that Tanja, Elly, and I can design the costumes for the show!"

"HOORAY!" her friends cheered.

Colette proudly showed off the sketches in the folder, which she, Tanja, and

I can't believe Ruby sabotaged Violet!
It's true.
Good news!

Elly had finished and colored in.

"These are great!" said Nicky.

"Can we CELEBRATE with you?" asked Shen.

He walked into the theater followed by Craig and Ryder. News had quickly spread that the three of them had passed the ACTING audition.

"We heard about your comedy routine," Pam said. "Is it true that you didn't know anything about it, Craig?"

Craig nodded. "Yeah, I had no idea. At first I was upset, but I understand that Ryder and Shen did this to help me." He turned to his two friends. "Just don't ever do that again!"

"We won't!" Ryder and Shen promised.

Nicky looked at Craig. "So, are you going to try out for the dance audition next?"

"NOOOOO! DON'T EVEN TALK ABOUT IT!"

Craig replied stubbornly.

"But you're a great dancer!" Pam told him. "You'll pass that audition for sure."

"Definitely!" Craig agreed. "But then I'll still have to go through the singing audition, and I just can't do that. I get really nervous, for some reason, and my voice cracks. It's too **embarrassing**!"

A SLIPPERY PLAN

The next day, all of the students who had passed the first audition gathered in the dance studio. A nervous vibe filled the room as everyone warmed up for the dance audition.

In the back of the room, Ruby and her friends whispered to one another.

"We will DEFINITELY slay this dance audition," she confidently told the Ruby Crew. "But we still need to make sure Paulina and Nicky get eliminated. And I know just how to do it!"

She took a sparkly jar out of her bag. The label read "Flashyfur Paw Polish."

"My mother invented this cream,"

Ruby explained. "It's a moisturizing paw cream, and it's super **GREASY**. So all we have to do is smear some on Paulina's and Nicky's dance shoes —"

"— and they'll **FALL** flat on their snouts!" Connie finished with a grin.

She and Zoe looked

at each other and **nodded**. While Nicky and Paulina were talking to Ryder, Connie and Zoe **SMEARED** the cream on their shoes.

Paulina and Nicky had no idea!

"Is Craig coming?" Paulina asked Ryder.

Ryder frowned. “I tried to convince him, but he wouldn’t come,” he replied. “He says it doesn’t matter, because he won’t do the singing audition anyway.”

“I feel bad for him,” said Nicky. “There has to be some way we can help him with his singing.”

“Sometimes it’s easier to HELP someone else than to be helped,” Paulina said thoughtfully.

Ryder looked amazed. “Paulina, you gave me a great idea,” he said. “Thanks! Be right back!”

Ryder RUSHED out of the dance studio.

I’ll just tell Craig that I need his help with my audition, he told himself as he ran. *Knowing him, he won’t say* **NO***!*

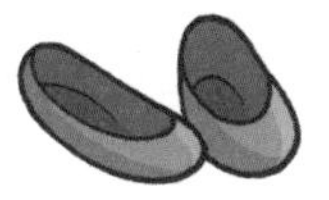

NICKY TAKES A TUMBLE

Ruby and her crew auditioned first, performing a perfectly synchronized dance routine.

"**PASS!**" said Professor Plié.

Next, it was Paulina's turn. She turned on the music: a **mellow** piece that she used to listen to back in **Peru**, with her little sister, Maria.

Ruby approached her. "Paulina, you forgot your ballet **shoes**!"

"Thanks, but I

don't need them," Paulina replied. "This dance works best if I perform it with bare paws."

RUBY WAS FURIOUS!

Paulina launched into her dance, spinning and jumping beautifully.

Professor Plié clapped her paws. "PASS!"

Then Ryder came back, dragging an unwilling Craig with him. But Ryder put on a hip-hop song, and as soon as Craig heard the music he got into it. He and Ryder BUSTED OUT their best moves.

"Great ENERGY! You both pass!" announced Professor Plié.

Craig just shook his head. "Thanks, but this is the end of auditions for me. I'm not going to sing!"

He left the dance hall, sulking, and Ryder went after him.

"All right, Nicky, it's your turn," announced Professor Plié.

Nicky pulled on her red ballet shoes. Her paws were shaking, and she realized she was a little nervous. The music started to play, and she stepped out onto the dance floor . . .

The SUPER-GREASY cream on the shoes worked! Nicky fell. Paulina rushed to her and helped her up.

"Nicky, are you OKAY?" she asked.

Nicky stepped on her ankle and winced. "I think I twisted my ankle," she said. "I don't know how I slipped like that!"

Professor Plié was concerned. "Nicky, I'm sorry, but I can't let you audition if you're hurt. I hope you understand."

Nicky nodded. "Yes, I do," she said, but she was holding back TEARS.

HELP, THEA SISTERS!

Feeling discouraged, Paulina and Nicky made their way to the theater later that day. Nicky could walk just fine, but her chance to perform in the musical was over.

Inside the theater, they found Colette, Elly, Tanja, and Violet hard at work on the COSTUMES. Mannequins were draped with fabric of all shapes and colors. Colette was patiently STITCHING orange and yellow crepe-paper strips onto the sleeves of the SCARECROW'S costume.

Violet attached aluminum FOIL to the Tin Man's costume. Tanja and Elly were using wool yarn to make the Cowardly Lion's mane. Behind them, Pam was painting the set to look like the **Emerald City**.

"Nicky, we heard about what happened," said Colette. "How **AWFUL**!"

"Well, the good news is that I can help you with the costumes now," Nicky replied.

Tanja handed her the strands of yarn. "Here, you can help us with the **MANE**. Sit down and take the weight off your ankle."

Nicky gratefully sat down on the stage while Paulina grabbed a paintbrush and helped Pam.

"There was something **GREASY** on the bottom of my ballet shoes," Nicky explained. "I'm pretty sure that Ruby's to blame, but I can't **PROVE** it."

"Another **trick** from Ruby?" Pam asked angrily. "This has to stop!"

Shen walked in, carrying a **toolbox** for Pam. "Yeah, it's not right what Ruby and

Another trick from Ruby?

her friends are doing," he said. "She keeps bragging that she'll get the starring role and nobody can stop her."

Paulina sighed. "She has been knocking us out of the competition, one by one. I wonder what she has planned for me tomorrow?"

"Don't worry," said Colette. "Your singing is stronger than any trick."

"And we'll help you," Nikki said.

"That's what we're here for," said Pam with a nod. "We're the Thea Sisters! We're BFFs forever. BEST FURRY FRIENDS!"

Violet giggled. "That's right!"

"Group hug!" shouted Paulina, and they all gathered in a tight circle.

"Friends forever!" they cried.

"Hey, glad I found you!" a voice called from the theater door. They all turned to

see Ryder. "I'm hoping you all can help me. Craig **PASSED** the first two auditions, but he's refusing to do the singing audition."

"Yes, we know," said Nicky.

"So what can we do?" Ryder asked. "He'd be great in the musical. For some reason, he gets super **embarrassed** when he sings, and his voice **cracks**."

"I've heard him sing in the SHOWER," Shen said. "His voice doesn't crack then."

Violet looked thoughtful for a moment. Then her face LIT UP. "I have an **idea**!" she cried. "I know how we can get Craig

to audition without being too scared . . . and I think we can outsmart Ruby at the same time."

Everyone leaned in closer to hear Violet's plan.

MISSION: HELP CRAIG!

The next morning, Craig walked into the theater at eight o'clock sharp. The room was completely DARK, except for one small spotlight shining on the center of the stage.

"HELLO?" he called out. "Anybody there?"

He scratched his head, worried. Ryder had texted him early, asking him to come to the stage to help move some of the scenery around. But where was he?

Then Paulina stepped out of the shadows on the

stage. "Hello, Craig!" she greeted him cheerfully. She held a sheet of music in her paw. "Why are you here so early?"

Relieved to see someone, Craig walked up to meet her.

"Ryder said he needed somebody strong to help out, and since I've got the muscles . . ." He winked jokingly at Paulina and squeezed his biceps.

Ha, ha, ha!

I've got the muscles!

Paulina laughed. "Maybe he's running late," she said. "Would you mind helping me in the meantime?"

"Sure," said Craig. "What can I do?"

"Well, I'm auditioning for

Dorothy's part, but this song is a duet," she said, holding up the music sheet. "Could you practice with me? It would really help to hear someone sing the other part."

Craig hesitated. "Well, I mean . . . I don't usually sing in front of —"

"It's just the two of us," Paulina said. "And it's just practice."

Craig relaxed a little. "Okay, I guess. Let me see it."

Paulina held out the music, and she began the song. Craig joined in when it came time. His voice did CRACK at first, but the more he sang, the more CONFIDENT he got. Deep and in tune, his voice echoed around the dark auditorium.

Soon, Paulina and Craig's voices were entwined in beautiful harmony. They both smiled. They sounded great together!

Craig forgot all about being nervous. He really got into it!

When they finished the song, applause filled the auditorium.

CLAP! CLAP! CLAP! CLAP!

Craig looked around, panicked, and stuttered. "B-but wh-who is there?"

Paulina smiled at him. "You were AMAZING!"

The lights of the stage came on, revealing Ryder, Shen, the other Thea Sisters, Tanja, and Elly sitting in the auditorium. Across the aisle from them sat Professor Plotfur, Professor Plié, and Professor Aria.

"That was a beautiful audition, you two," Professor Aria said, clapping her paws.

Craig was **STUNNED**. "So . . . did you guys all plan this?"

"That's right!" replied Ryder. "It was

Bravo!
B-but who is there?

Bravo!

Violet's idea. When we explained the issue, the professors were **happy** to help us."

Professor Aria nodded. "We wanted to be fair. It would be a shame if you had given up just because you were nervous. And now you know that you can do it!"

Craig smiled. "Yeah, I guess you're right!"

"I hope you're not **mad**," said Paulina.

Craig shook his head. "No way. You did me a favor."

The happy moment was interrupted by a shrieking voice that rang through the theater.

"WHAT IS GOING ON HERE?!"

BACK OFF, RUBY!

Ruby stormed into the theater like a **roll of thunder**, followed by Connie, Zoe, and Alicia.

"Is this a **special** audition?" she yelled. "Why didn't I know about it?"

Ruby was angry because Paulina had auditioned before she had a chance to sabotage her. She pointed **THREATENINGLY** at Paulina and Craig.

"This is unfair! You two should be **disqualified**!"

Shen reacted quickly. "**BACK OFF**, Ruby!" he yelled. He was fed up with her arrogant attitude. "You talk about fairness. But we all know that you **sabotaged** Nicky and Violet."

Ruby looked **SHOCKED**. Nobody had ever stood up to her like this before.

"If you really are **better** than everybody else, why don't you just prove it on the stage?" Shen continued. "Go ahead and **audition**!"

The professors had been listening intently. Professor Aria spoke up.

"It was our choice to let Craig audition this way," she said firmly. "Craig and Paulina have done nothing wrong. And I would be happy to hear you sing now, Ruby. Go ahead."

Ruby's CONFIDENCE drained right out of her. "Audition? Now?" she asked, turning to her friends for help.

But Zoe, Connie, and Alicia blushed, staring at the floor. They didn't know what to do! They had spent the night before plotting a new trick for Paulina. None of them had practiced a song for the audition.

A very **embarrassed** Ruby started walking backward toward the entrance.

"Um, I, uh, left my music in my room," she lied, trying to come up with an excuse.

"Thank you, but I prefer to audition later."

Then she QUICKLY left, followed by her friends.

A ROLE FOR EVERYONE

The singing auditions went on until noon. After lunch, the professors got together in the dance studio to talk about the casting of the show.

"**THE SUSPENSE IS TOO MUCH!**" Colette said dramatically as she waited in the hall with her friends.

Pam paced BACK and FORTH, munching on a cheese cracker. "They're taking forever!"

"How can you be so **calm**?" Violet asked Paulina.

Paulina smiled. "I don't know. I think Craig is the most NERVOUS one of all!"

Craig could not sit still! He kept

GETTING UP and *GOING* to eavesdrop at the door, and then he would sit down again.

He was more anxious than a rat at a cat party!

Finally, the door opened, and the professors came out with the cast list.

Professor Plotfur stepped forward and cleared his throat. "In the story of The

Wonderful Wizard of Oz, the character of the TIN MAN believes he does not have a heart. But while he looks STRONG and tough on the outside, he is sensitive on the inside. Therefore, this role will be played by . . . Craig!"

Craig looked SURPRISED, and then he smiled. Ryder slapped him on the back.

Professor Plié stepped forward next.

"The SCARECROW thinks he doesn't have any **brains**, but it's his good thinking that helps his friends out of tough times. Ryder helped Craig in the same way. The role goes to Ryder!"

Ryder smiled **happily** when he heard his name.

"The LION thinks he has no courage, but he BRAVELY stands up to defend others," she continued. "The role goes to Shen, who showed **STRENGTH** when he stood up for his friends."

The other students

surrounded the three boy mice, who, between **compliments** and pats on the shoulders, looked a little **dazed**.

Camille Ratyshnikov, head of the department, announced the **starring** role.

"The part of **Dorothy**, who finds her way back home with the support of her friends, goes to — Paulina!"

"**HOORAY!**" cheered the Thea Sisters.

There were still more roles to assign, and Professor Plotfur read those out loud. "Ruby, Zoe, Alicia, and Connie, each of you has a part in the musical."

Ruby had been looking **depressed** at losing the part of Dorothy, but she **perked up** when she heard this.

"I'm assuming these are **important** roles, Professor?" she asked.

"Indeed they are," Professor Plotfur

replied. "You, Ruby, have proven that you want to win at all costs."

Ruby nodded. That was certainly true.

"And Alicia, Connie, and Zoe, you have shown that you are willing to follow Ruby's every move — both on the dance floor and off," Professor Aria continued.

The Ruby Crew members looked at one another, confused.

"That's why we think that Ruby would make a perfect WICKED WITCH OF THE WEST, and the rest of you can be her loyal assistants, the WINGED MONKEYS!" Professor Aria concluded.

Ruby's face turned PALE as mozzarella and then flushed red with anger.

"Wicked witch!" she screeched. "Who are you calling wicked?"

Some of the students giggled. Ruby

sounded **WICKED**, squeaking like that!

Colette tried to make her feel better. "Look, we've designed some spectacular costumes for you," she said, showing her the drawings.

But Ruby was horrified. "**Garbage bags**? You want me to wear a dress made of black garbage bags?"

"It's a very witchy outfit," Colette explained.

"And what's with these monkey outfits?" Connie complained. "Look at those fake feathers! We'll look like CHICKENS."

Nicky and Violet could not help it; they burst out laughing.

"Serves them right for sabotaging us like that!" Nicky whispered to her friend.

"They are their own worst enemies," said Violet. "They should be **happy** that they got roles in the show. Instead, they're miserable!"

TOGETHER ONSTAGE!

The next month was a whirlwind as the Thea Sisters prepared for the show. They met every day in the theater for rehearsal after their classes were over. Most days they stayed LATE into the night, with only a quick break.

Paulina was always the first one to get there. She would walk around backstage with her **camera** around her neck, ready to capture the most important and funniest moments of that fabumouse experience!

Craig had lost most of

his nervousness and really **enjoyed** the rehearsals. Every once in a while, though, his voice would get **Shaky** and **CRACK**. Then he would have to start all over from the beginning.

"That's enough!" Ruby complained one day. "How did you ever get a singing role

when your voice keeps cracking? We should call you the Shaky Tin Man."

Craig **blushed**, embarrassed, but Ryder jumped in to help.

"Then you should be called the Late Witch, right, Ruby?" he asked.

"You're always late for rehearsal and make everyone wait!" Shen added. "It's really pretty rude."

Ruby raised her snout in the air. "A real diva knows how to keep everyone in suspense," she said.

Ruby didn't know it yet, but that attitude was about to get her in trouble on opening night.

While the other performers gathered backstage, eager for the show to start, Ruby holed up in her dressing room. In true Ruby fashion, she had hired a professional makeup artist and wanted to make a grand entrance.

As Ruby got made up, the journalists her mother had called arrived and started interviewing everybody. But by the time Ruby was finished, they had all taken their seats. The show was about to start and there was no time to interview her!

The LIGHTS dimmed in the theater, and the audience grew silent. Everything was in place. The members of the cast formed a circle and put their PAWS together.

"Places, everyone!" Professor Plotfur whispered.

Paulina stepped out onto the darkened stage, her heart beating quickly from the excitement. The thick red CURTAINS opened up, and a spotlight shone on her. The audience burst into applause.

THE SHOW HAD BEGUN!

A GIFT FOR MARIA

One month later, in a town far away from Whale Island, a postmouse delivered a nicely wrapped PACKET to the paws of an excited and curious little mouselet.

The **lucky** recipient was Maria*, Paulina's little sister!

*Read more about her in the Thea Sisters book *Thea Stilton and the Secret City*.

Paulina had been on cloud nine since starring as Dorothy in *The Wonderful Wizard of Oz*. Headmaster de Mousus had personally CONGRATULATED her. The school NEWSPAPER had interviewed her. Even hard-to-please Professor Ratyshnikov had complimented her.

WHAT A FEELING!

Paulina wanted to dedicate her success to her favorite rodent in the world: her little sister, Maria! She packed up all the PHOTOS that had been taken during rehearsals, along with a long letter.

Maria started reading right away . . .

Dear Little Sister,

The musical *The Wonderful Wizard of Oz* was a real success! I so wished I could have seen you in the audience, but with this letter I'll tell you all about it, as if you had been right there with me.

To play Dorothy's part, I had to go through three difficult auditions: drama, singing, and dancing. Thankfully, the Thea Sisters were there to support me all the way. They send you hugs!

Colette and Violet worked on the costumes with our friends

Tanja and Elly. The finished costumes were mousetastic!

Pam was in charge of the lighting and set design, and Nicky helped her. They created some really spectacular special effects.

Pamela looked really confident behind the backstage control panel. During rehearsal, she kept repeating, "Nobody will end up in the dark as long as I have the controls!"

But the biggest surprises might have been Craig, Ryder, and Shen.

Craig was embarrassed to sing in public and his voice would crack. But he got more comfortable onstage the more he practiced. On opening night, he sounded amazing! Shen was a big hit, too. He looked so sweet in his lion costume, but during rehearsal he was able

to prove that he could roar loudly when he needed to.

And Ryder is normally so quiet and shy! Well, he really got into his role as the carefree Scarecrow. During rehearsal, he was always joking around and singing.

When the show ended, he went right back into his shell, which is a shame. But he is an honest and gentle soul – and the complete opposite of his sister, Ruby! She never fails to show us her true colors. She always got to rehearsal late and was always in a bad mood.

She even managed to arrive late on opening night! When she walked out onstage, though, she was very focused and did her best. She was perfect in the part of the Wicked Witch of the West!

Professor Plotfur himself played the

Wonderful Wizard of Oz. He's a great actor! And Professor Aria lent her amazing singing voice to the role of the good witch who helped Dorothy. She was perfect for the part!

On opening night, everything went exactly like a dream. For a moment, onstage, I really felt like Dorothy, far away from home and wandering around in a big, wonderful, fabumouse world.

Luckily, my friends are with me, and inside my heart, I always know how to find the path to bring me back to you!

Please, Little Sister, take good care of the most precious memento from this show. You will find it inside this package. It is a framed photo of everyone who worked on the show!

With love and a kiss on the tip of your nose,

Paulina

Don't miss any of these Mouseford Academy adventures!

#1 Drama at Mouseford

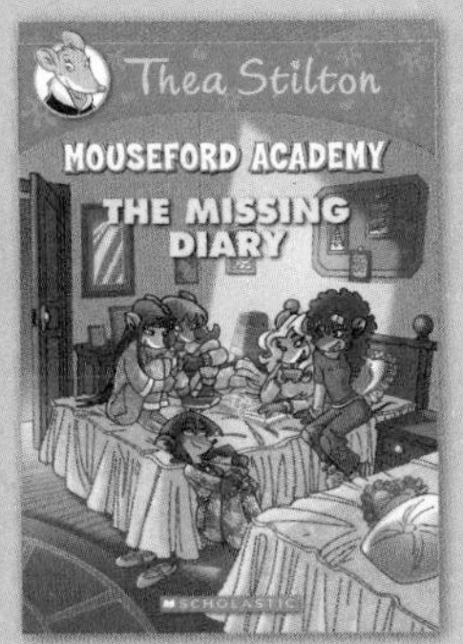

#2 The Missing Diary

#3 Mouselets in Danger

#4 Dance Challenge

#5 The Secret Invention

#6 A Mouseford Musical

Don't miss these exciting Thea Sisters adventures!

Thea Stilton and the Dragon's Code

Thea Stilton and the Mountain of Fire

Thea Stilton and the Ghost of the Shipwreck

Thea Stilton and the Secret City

Thea Stilton and the Mystery in Paris

Thea Stilton and the Cherry Blossom Adventure

Thea Stilton and the Star Castaways

Thea Stilton: Big Trouble in the Big Apple

Thea Stilton and the Ice Treasure

Thea Stilton and the Secret of the Old Castle

Thea Stilton and the Blue Scarab Hunt

Thea Stilton and the Prince's Emerald

Thea Stilton and the Mystery on the Orient Express

Thea Stilton and the Dancing Shadows

Thea Stilton and the Legend of the Fire Flowers

Thea Stilton and the Spanish Dance Mission

Thea Stilton and the Journey to the Lion's Den

Thea Stilton and the Great Tulip Heist

Thea Stilton and the Chocolate Sabotage

Thea Stilton and the Missing Myth

Thea Stilton and the Lost Letters

#21 The Wild, Wild West

#22 The Secret of Cacklefur Castle

A Christmas Tale

#23 Valentine's Day Disaster

#24 Field Trip to Niagara Falls

#25 The Search for Sunken Treasure

#26 The Mummy with No Name

#27 The Christmas Toy Factory

#28 Wedding Crasher

#29 Down and Out Down Under

#30 The Mouse Island Marathon

#31 The Mysterious Cheese Thief

Christmas Catastrophe

#32 Valley of the Giant Skeletons

#33 Geronimo and the Gold Medal Mystery

#34 Geronimo Stilton, Secret Agent

#35 A Very Merry Christmas

#36 Geronimo's Valentine

#37 The Race Across America

#38 A Fabumouse School Adventure

#39 Singing Sensation

#40 The Karate Mouse

#41 Mighty Mount Kilimanjaro

#42 The Peculiar Pumpkin Thief

#43 I'm Not a Supermouse!

#44 The Giant Diamond Robbery

#45 Save the White Whale!

#46 The Haunted Castle

#47 Run for the Hills, Geronimo!

#48 The Mystery in Venice

#49 The Way of the Samurai

#50 This Hotel Is Haunted!

#51 The Enormouse Pearl Heist

#52 Mouse in Space!

#53 Rumble in the Jungle

#54 Get into Gear, Stilton!

#55 The Golden Statue Plot

#56 Flight of the Red Bandit

The Hunt for the Golden Book

#57 The Stinky Cheese Vacation

#58 The Super Chef Contest

#59 Welcome to Moldy Manor

The Hunt for the Curious Cheese

#60 The Treasure of Easter Island

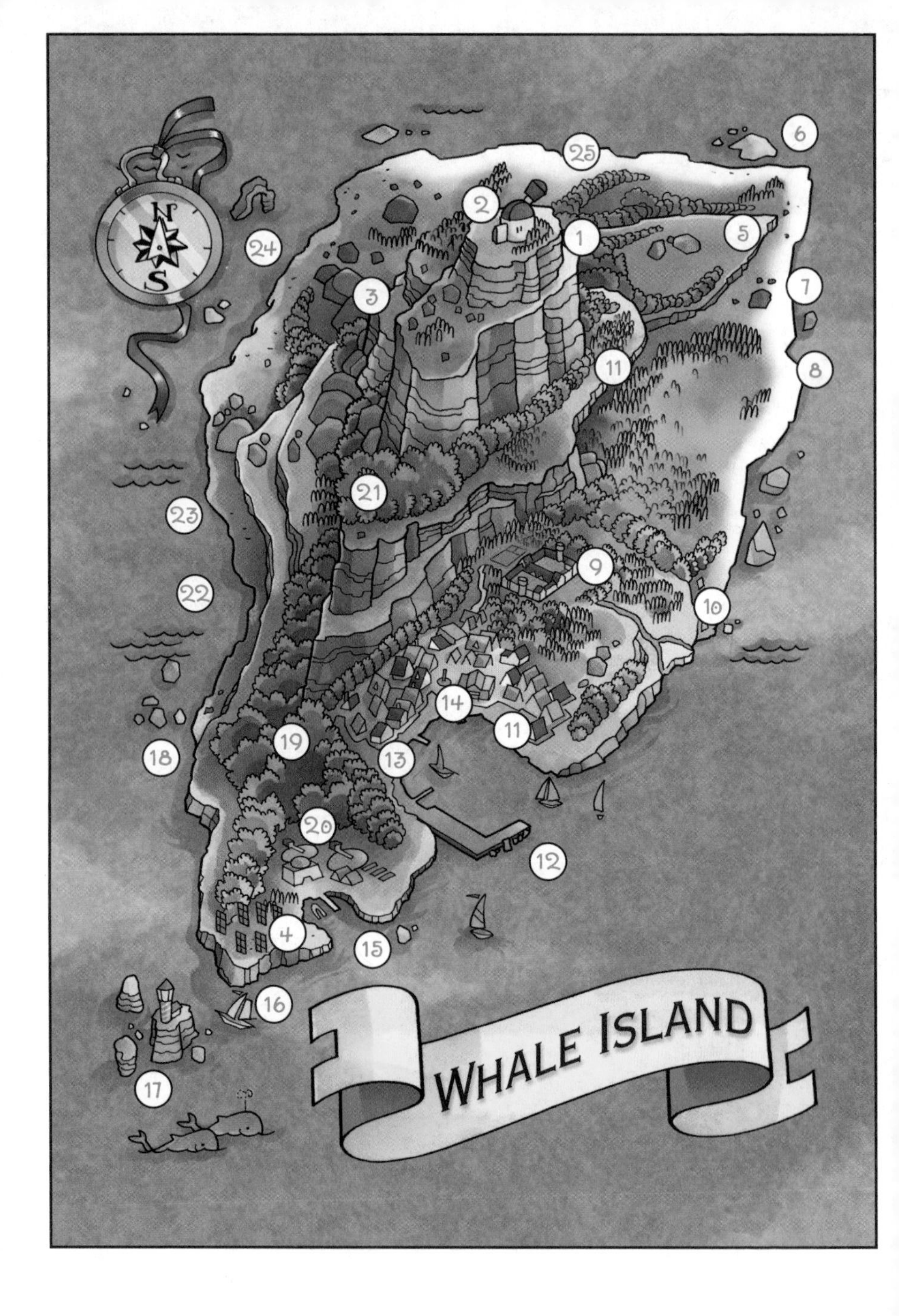
N
S
1
2
3
4
5
6
7
8
9
10
11
11
12
13
14
15
16
17
18
19
20
21
22
23
24
25
WHALE ISLAND

MAP OF WHALE ISLAND

1. Falcon Peak
2. Observatory
3. Mount Landslide
4. Solar Energy Plant
5. Ram Plain
6. Very Windy Point
7. Turtle Beach
8. Beachy Beach
9. Mouseford Academy
10. Kneecap River
11. Mariner's Inn
12. Port
13. Squid House
14. Town Square
15. Butterfly Bay
16. Mussel Point
17. Lighthouse Cliff
18. Pelican Cliff
19. Nightingale Woods
20. Marine Biology Lab
21. Hawk Woods
22. Windy Grotto
23. Seal Grotto
24. Seagulls Bay
25. Seashell Beach

THANKS FOR READING, AND GOOD-BYE UNTIL OUR NEXT ADVENTURE!